The Very Fairy Princess

Attitude of Gratitude

by Julie Andrews & Emma Walton Hamilton

Illustrated by
Christine Davenier

Little, Brown and Company
New York   Boston

Hooray! It's Gratitude Day!
At school, we'll be practicing an Attitude of Gratitude
by showing kindness and appreciation all day long!
Well…NO ONE has a fuller heart or is more appreciative
than a fairy princess.
That's me! Gerry, the VERY fairy princess.

This is going to be the SPARKLIEST day!
We're supposed to celebrate everyone and everything we're grateful
for by giving TONS of compliments and thanks.
Gratitude Day is also about helping others, so we're bringing in donations
for our local food pantry. I hope they like sprinkles as much as I do!

In the afternoon, we're having an art show. Our paintings will be
sold to support the Animal Welfare Center.

I have to give MYSELF a compliment, because I think my painting is
the BEST I've ever done!

(Fairy princesses always rise to the occasion for a needy cause.)

I stuff my backpack with schoolwork, my sprinkles, and a can of beans that Daddy is donating to the food drive.

I gobble my breakfast, hug Mommy and Daddy,
and high-five my brother, Stewart.

My Attitude of Gratitude is off to a great start!

When the school bus arrives, I give our driver an EXTRA-sparkly smile and look for my best friend, Delilah.

"She's absent," says Connor, who is sitting in her seat. "Delilah has poison ivy. I bet she looks like a big red tomato!"
"That is NOT a compliment," I say.

The bus lurches forward, and I have to sit next to him.
This strains my Gratitude Attitude.

Poor Delilah!
She'll miss all the fun, I'll miss her at school,
and the food pantry will miss her delicious tomatoes!

But it's Gratitude Day, so I have to focus on the positive.
(Fairy princesses hold their heads high, even in the face
of disappointment.)

Our teacher, Mr. Bonario, tells us to put our donations on the table.
I open my backpack and reach for my jar of sprinkles.

OH NO! The top has come loose, and sprinkles are EVERYWHERE!
An empty jar of sprinkles is like a box without a present!

Cody Rose taps my shoulder. "I have some extra bags of gummy bears," she says. "Would you like to put them in your jar?"

I almost BURST with gratitude!
"Thank you, Cody Rose!" I say, then add a compliment.
"You're a kind friend."

Our Gratitude Attitudes are outstanding during history, English, and even math.

But in science class, a TERRIBLE noise blares through the classroom.

"Fire drill!" says Mr. Bonario. "Everybody, line up for the playground!"
I am the first one to reach the door!
(If there's anything that robs a fairy princess of her sparkle,
it's a FIRE DRILL!)

The siren is quieter outside, but now we have to wait
on the playground and be counted.
An Attitude of Gratitude is not easy when
your heart is pounding and your ears are ringing!
"Let's try something fun!" says Mr. Bonario.
He lifts my arms above my head and says,
"Hold that pose."

Then he puts everyone else in different positions. What is he up to?

"Now, don't move," he says. "And…SMILE!" He snaps a bunch of photos.

"Let's see! Let's see!" we all shout.

"Later!" He winks. "It's time to go to the art show."

We file into the Great Hall, where our paintings are on display.

They ALL show things we're grateful for, but each one is different.

Patrick drew himself reaching up to the sun.

José painted someone hugging a tree full of flowers.

I compliment them both on their excellent artwork.

Delilah painted two friends holding hands. It must be me and her,

because one of them is wearing a crown!

I'll have to give her an EXTRA compliment when she comes back to school.

Connor points to a picture on the wall. "Your clown rocks!" he says.
The painting looks familiar. I squint and tilt my head.

GERRY

"It's NOT a clown!" I wail. "It's a CORNUCOPIA!
And it's hanging sideways!"

This day is a DISASTER! My best friend is absent,
my sprinkles exploded, we had a fire alarm, and
now my finest painting has been DISGRACED!

My Attitude of Gratitude flies out the window, and I burst into tears.
(Even a fairy princess can crumble under EXTREME pressure!)

"What's a cornucopia?" says Connor.

Mr. Bonario puts an arm around my shoulder.

"It's a symbol of abundance—a horn of plenty.

Gerry has created TWO paintings in one! I'll have to buy that

and hang it in my office."

I blink, and my Gratitude Attitude zooms back like a boomerang!
(No one appreciates a compliment more than a fairy princess.)

When we get back to our classroom, there's a surprise waiting. The photographs Mr. Bonario took on the playground are posted on the wall.

We suddenly notice that our poses spell out two words: THANK YOU!

"Thank YOU, Mr. Bonario!" we all shout.

"You're a GREAT teacher!" I add.

(Fairy princesses always go the extra distance.)

That night at dinner, I tell Mommy, Daddy, and Stewart all about my day. "Delilah was absent and my sprinkles exploded, but Cody Rose came to the rescue," I say.

"And there was a fire drill, but it gave us a GREAT class photo. My painting was hanging sideways in the art show, but it turned out twice as nice that way! And we all shared the BEST compliments."

"Sounds like a GRATIFYING day," says Daddy.

"Why don't we share our own compliments?"
Mommy suggests. "Your dinner was delicious, dear."

"Thank you," says Daddy. "Stewart, your trumpet playing has really improved!" Stewart grins, then looks at me.

"You're an okay sister," he says.

"Even if you are a fairy princess."

I feel SUPER sparkly…and I know just what to say.

"THANK YOU, ALL…for being the BEST family
a fairy princess could ever have!"

For Alison Cordaro—with love and gratitude.

—J.A. & E.W.H.

For Allison Moore, with all my gratitude for her help so precious!

—C.D.

About This Book

The illustrations for this book were done in ink and color pencil on Keaykolour paper.
The text was set in Baskerville and the display type is Mayfair.
This book was edited by Lisa Yoskowitz and designed by Aram Kim with art direction by Saho Fujii.
The production was supervised by Erika Schwartz, and the production editor was Wendy Dopkin.